Dear Parent:
Your child's love of reading starts here!

Every child learns to read in a different way and at his or her own speed. Some go back and forth between reading levels and read favorite books again and again. Others read through each level in order. You can help your young reader improve and become more confident by encouraging his or her own interests and abilities. From books your child reads with you to the first books he or she reads alone, there are I Can Read Books for every stage of reading:

SHARED READING
Basic language, word repetition, and whimsical illustrations, ideal for sharing with your emergent reader

BEGINNING READING
Short sentences, familiar words, and simple concepts for children eager to read on their own

READING WITH HELP
Engaging stories, longer sentences, and language play for developing readers

READING ALONE
Complex plots, challenging vocabulary, and high-interest topics for the independent reader

I Can Read Books have introduced children to the joy of reading since 1957. Featuring award-winning authors and illustrators and a fabulous cast of beloved characters, I Can Read Books set the standard for beginning readers.

A lifetime of discovery begins with the magical words "I Can Read!"

Visit www.icanread.com for information
on enriching your child's reading experience.

To all the little girls who dream big—keep dreaming!
—*K. D. & S. R. J.*

For Gerry—We love and miss you!
—*J. M.*

The full-color artwork was created digitally.

I Can Read® and I Can Read Book® are trademarks of HarperCollins Publishers.

Vivi Loves Science: Sink or Float. Text copyright © 2022 by Kimberly Derting and Shelli R. Johannes. Illustrations copyright © 2022 by Joelle Murray. All rights reserved. No part of this book may be used or reproduced in any manner whatsoever without written permission except in the case of brief quotations embodied in critical articles and reviews. Printed in the USA. For information address HarperCollins Children's Books, a division of HarperCollins Publishers, 195 Broadway, New York, NY 10007.
www.icanread.com

Library of Congress Cataloging-in-Publication Data is available.
ISBN 978-0-06-311657-3 (hardcover) — ISBN 978-0-06-311656-6 (paperback)

22 23 24 25 26 LSCC 10 9 8 7 6 5 4 3 2 1   ❖   First Edition
🏮 Greenwillow Books

n Read!

Vivi
LOVES SCIENCE

Sink or Float

By KIMBERLY DERTING
and SHELLI R. JOHANNES
pictures by JOELLE MURRAY

Greenwillow Books
An Imprint of HarperCollins*Publishers*

Vivi jumped out of bed.

She fed her goldfish, Bubbles.

"I am going to the aquarium today,"

Vivi said to Bubbles.

"I will see lots of fish,

but you'll always be my favorite!"

The school bus dropped everyone off at the aquarium.

"Let's go learn about different marine animals," said Ms. Cousteau, Vivi's science teacher.

Vivi loved marine biology.

She could not wait to meet

the marine biologist at the aquarium.

Vivi had a list of questions ready!

First, the class touched the stingrays.
Vivi was surprised to feel the rough texture
of their skin.

Next, the class observed the sea lions.

Vivi didn't know sea lions could swim so fast.

Then they visited the sea turtles.

One turtle was at least seventy-five years old.

The class gathered at the tropical tank.
The tank was filled with fish and marine
animals in all shapes, sizes, and colors.
A group of bright-blue fish swirled by.

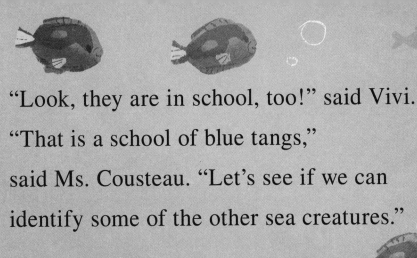

"Look, they are in school, too!" said Vivi.

"That is a school of blue tangs,"
said Ms. Cousteau. "Let's see if we can
identify some of the other sea creatures."

"I see an octopus,"
Graeme said.
"There is a clownfish,"
Vivi said. "They hide in
sea anemones."

"Wow! That hammerhead shark is huge," Graeme said.

"Sharks don't have to hide from anything," Vivi said.

Graeme pointed at a fish resting in the sand.
"Is there something wrong with that one?"
he asked.

"No, that's a flounder," Ms. Cousteau said.

"Aren't fish supposed to swim?"
asked Graeme.

"A flounder is a species of flatfish,"
said Ms. Cousteau.

"It can swim, but it likes to sink into the sand
and hide."

"What makes a fish sink or float?"
asked Vivi.

"Good question," Ms. Cousteau said.

"Let's ask Dr. Fisher."

She smiled at the scientist who had joined
them at the tank.

"Dr. Fisher is a marine biologist,"
said Ms. Cousteau.
"She studies the ocean and everything
that lives in it."
This was exactly what Vivi
had been waiting for!

17

"Does anyone know why fish sink or float?" asked Dr. Fisher.

"Is it because of their fins?" said Vivi.

"Good guess!" said Dr. Fisher.

"But it's because of a special organ called a swim bladder."

"What is that?" asked Mia.

"A swim bladder
is an inflatable sac
that fills with air,
sort of like our lungs,
or a balloon,"
said Dr. Fisher.

"Let's go to the lab and
make our own swim
bladders, so you can
see how they work."
Dr. Fisher smiled and
led the way.

"This is going to be fun!"
Vivi said to Graeme.

19

Dr. Fisher drew a diagram
on the whiteboard in her lab.
"Whether an object sinks or floats depends
a lot on its density," she said.
"Do you mean how heavy it is?" Vivi asked.

"Actually, density is both how heavy and how big an object is," said Dr. Fisher.

"So a brick would have a high density," said Vivi.

"And a beach ball has a low density!" said Graeme. "That's right!" said Dr. Fisher.

"The swim bladder helps the fish change its density," said Dr. Fisher.

"Which helps it sink or float!" said Vivi.

Dr. Fisher nodded.

"Exactly. Let's see how it works."

Dr. Fisher handed out the worksheets for the experiment.

"Use the materials at your station," she said. "Let's investigate!"

Vivi and her team followed the lab instructions.

Vivi pushed one end of
a long plastic tube through
the opening of the balloon.

Graeme taped
it up tight.

Mia put the balloon into
a glass bottle.

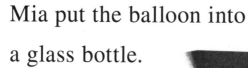

Benji taped the tube
to the bottle opening.

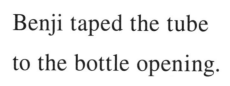

24

"What do you think will happen when you put your bottle in the water?" asked Dr. Fisher.

"Will it sink or float?"

"The glass feels heavy, so I bet it will sink," said Mia.

Vivi put their bottle
into the tub.

The bottle filled
with water and
sank to the bottom.

"Does anyone know
why the bottle sank?"
asked Dr. Fisher.

26

"Because our balloon is empty!" Vivi said.

"Good observation!" said Dr. Fisher.

"The bottle filled with water
when you put it into the tub."

"It was too dense to float," said Graeme.

"You got it!"
said Dr. Fisher.

"What do you think will happen if we inflate the balloon?" said Dr. Fisher.

"Let's find out!" Graeme said. Benji blew into the tube. Air filled the balloon.

As the balloon grew, the bottle rose to the surface.

"It's floating!" said Graeme.

"That's because the air in the balloon is much lighter than the water," said Dr. Fisher.

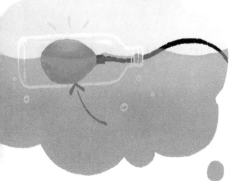

"So the bottle is not as dense anymore!" said Vivi.

"Let's deflate the balloon and see what happens," Graeme said.

Benji uncovered the tube, and the air started to escape.

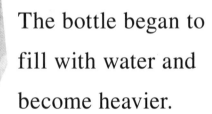

The bottle began to fill with water and become heavier.

"Look. It is sinking again," said Vivi.

"Can you see how this activity mimics a fish?" Dr. Fisher asked.

"Now it looks like a flounder," said Graeme.

"I get it!" Vivi said. "The bottle is our fish."

"And the balloon is its swim bladder," Benji said.

"Which helps it sink or float!" said Mia.

"I wonder if all fish have swim bladders,"
Vivi said.

"Actually, sharks and some stingrays
don't have swim bladders," said Dr. Fisher.
"It's a good question. You would make
a great marine biologist."

Vivi smiled.

"I have more questions," she said.

"Let's hear them," said Dr. Fisher.

Vivi read her list of questions.

Dr. Fisher answered them one by one.

"I had no idea fish were so amazing,"
Graeme said.

"They're not," Vivi said. "They're fintastic!

Do fish get sunburned? Yes!

Why do fish float? Swim Bladder!

Do all fish need gills? Yes!

Is a seahorse a fish? Yes!

What is the smallest fish? Dwarf Minnow!

Can starfish swim? NO - they glide.

Is an electric eel really electric? Yes!

Do flying fish really fly? Sort of - they also glide.

That night at home, Vivi observed Bubbles swimming around the tank.

"Now I know why you can float," she said.

Vivi loved science and marine biology.

But she loved Bubbles even more.

Vivi
LOVES SCIENCE

Make Your Own Swim Bladder

In this experiment, the bottle mimics the body of the fish, and the balloon is like the fish's swim bladder.

Materials

- Small glass bottle
- A balloon that fits inside the bottle
- Plastic tubing (at least 12 inches long)

- Strong waterproof tape
- A sink, bucket, or waterproof container big enough so the bottle can float freely

Prepare your swim bladder

1. Fill your container with water.

2. Push one end of the plastic tube through the opening of the balloon.

3. Tape the balloon and the tube together, creating a seal. Make sure the connection is airtight.

4. Put the balloon inside the glass bottle and tape the tube to the bottle opening.

38

Make your swim bladder sink or float

1. Place the bottle with the balloon inside
   of it into the container
   of water.

2. Now, carefully blow into
   the tube, so the balloon inside
   the bottle starts to inflate.

3. Next, inflate the balloon
   until it almost fills
   the whole bottle.

4. Let the balloon
   deflate again.

Experiment with inflating and deflating the balloon
and observe what happens to the bottle.

Results

What happens when the bottle fills up with water? Why?

What happens when you inflate the balloon with air? Why?

What happens when you let the air out of the balloon? Why?

Having fun with Sink and Float

Get a bowl or a bucket and fill it with water.
Collect some objects around the house or garden.

Drop your objects in the water.
Do they sink or float?

A rock	A leaf	A crayon

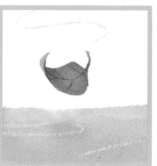

Sink or float?	Sink or float?	Sink or float?

Do you know why an object sinks or floats?

It's all about density. Objects that sink are denser than water.
Objects that float are less dense than water.

Glossary

Density: A measurement that compares the amount of matter an object has to its volume. An object with a lot of matter in a certain volume has a high density.

Float: To rest in or on the surface of a liquid or water.

Marine biology: The study of any plant or animal that lives in the ocean.

Sink: To move or drop down in liquid or water.